WILLIAM
~ HEADS TO ~
# HOLLYWOOD

INTERNATIONAL
CAT OF MYSTERY

HELEN HANCOCKS

This book is dedicated to my grandma. With love and thanks. H.H.

A TEMPLAR BOOK

First published in the UK in 2015 by Templar Publishing,
an imprint of the Bonnier Company Limited,
Deepdene Lodge, Deepdene Avenue, Dorking, Surrey, RH5 4AT, UK
www.templarco.co.uk

10 9 8 7 6 5 4 3 2 1

ISBN 978-1-78370-274-9 (hardback)
ISBN 978-1-78370-333-3 (paperback)

Edited by Zanna Davidson

Printed in China

WILLIAM
HEADS TO
HOLLYWOOD

HELEN HANCOCKS

templar publishing

William, international cat of mystery, was bored. Recently, all his cases had been getting silly and rather too easy to solve.

Just the other week, he had to find a man's missing hat.

It turned out to be on the man's head.

William was beginning to despair
of ever cracking another major case...

...when a perfumed letter arrived for him.

It was from Audrey Mieowski, the loveliest star in Tinseltown!

Dear William,

I need your help! The statues for the Golden Cuckoo Awards have been stolen and the ceremony is tomorrow night. It's a highly suspicious case and you are the cat to solve it.

Don your detective hat and meet me at the airport.

Yours,

Audrey Mieowski

This was the case he'd been waiting for...
William was heading to HOLLYWOOD.

He catnapped the whole way there.

ARRIVALS

WILLIAM
INTERNATIONAL
CAT OF MYSTERY

Audrey was at the airport to meet him. She was even more dazzling than in her films.

"There's no time to lose," she said. "The Golden Cuckoos are the most important awards in Hollywood."

They sped off to the Cuckoo Studios – the scene of the crime.
"There were ten statues," explained Audrey, "and now they're all gone!"

Cuckoo Studios

STAGE 03

"Are there any suspects?" William asked.

"No, it could be anyone!"

William searched the scene for clues.

He found a hair pin...
and some blue feathers.

"These could be the leads we need to catch the thief!" exclaimed William.

The chase was on.

But first William needed lunch – a case was never solved on an empty stomach, so they headed straight to the studio canteen.

Just then, in burst Ms Vivienne Baxter, once the greatest star of them all. "Ah, you must be the cat who is solving the crime of the stolen statues. Who could do such a thing? Those poor darling Cuckoos! I wish you luck, Mister William." And out she swept.

"That's strange," mused Audrey,
"she's never even talked to me before.
Something fishy is going on. Let's be in
cahoots and crack this case together!"

It didn't take them long to track down
more of the blue feathers...

"Oh dear!" said William. "These feathers aren't the ones from the crime scene. They're much too long."

STAGE 12

STAGE 14

But up ahead was a set of footprints...

...which led the sleuthing cats straight onto the set of the latest Cuckoo western.

CUT !!

William was so busy following the footprints he collided with the costume rail.

"Aha!" he cried. "We've found our first statue."

"These costumes came straight from the props department," said Audrey.

"Then that's our next stop."

The props department
was crammed full of treasures.

William gazed around, spellbound.
How would they ever find
anything in here?

After hours of searching, William and Audrey
were no closer to finding the rest of the Golden Cuckoos.
"Oh fishsticks!" William exclaimed.
"I've failed to crack this case."

"Never give up," said Audrey.
"There's a big fancy dress party before the Golden Cuckoo Awards tonight.
Let's mingle with the stars and see if we can spot the culprit."

William had never seen anywhere so grand and palatial.

He was also highly impressed
with the canapés, and was just about
to ask for milk, frothed not stirred...

...when in walked
Vivienne Baxter.

There was something
strange yet familiar
about her outfit.
William couldn't
quite put his
paw on it.

The feathers in her scarf matched those at the crime scene... and the decoration in her hat looked rather like...

...a Golden Cuckoo!

"She's the thief!" he cried.

Ms Baxter looked up in alarm, and fled.

Audrey and William set off in hot pursuit...

speeding down the Hollywood Hills...

across Sunset Boulevard...

all the way out to Santa Monica Pier.

DONUTS

"Quick, there she is!" cried William. "Heading into the hall of mirrors..."

But Ms Baxter had vanished!
"Let's take the ferris wheel for a
better view," suggested Audrey.

From up high,
they could see Ms Baxter,
running to the end
of the pier.

DONUTS

"Stop!" they cried, as they raced after her.
"There's nowhere left to run. We know it was you."

"Yes," she cried. "I stole them ALL! But I deserved them.
And if I can't have them, no one can."

NOOOOOOo!!!

With those words,
Ms Baxter flung the statue into the sea.
Bravely, William leapt in after it.

"Oh, William," said Audrey, as she tossed him a lifebelt. "How heroic!"

"All I wanted was recognition," Ms Baxter confessed. "No one ever appreciated little old me. And if you meddling cats must know, the other eight are stashed at my mansion."

"I just wanted to be perfect!" she cried, as the police came to take her away.

William and Audrey raced to Ms Baxter's mansion.
"At last," said William. "We've cracked this case,
and just in time..."

...for the Golden Cuckoo Awards
to take place, with William
as guest of honour.

At the end of the ceremony, William was presented with an award of his very own...

The Golden Cuckoo for Best Cat Detective of the Year.

All too soon, it was time for William to bid Audrey farewell.

They both agreed it had been a beautiful partnership.

William's time in Hollywood was over...

BLACK CAT
AUDITIONS
THIS WAY.
YOUR CHANCE TO
STAR ALONGSIDE
AUDREY MIEOWSKI.
IN HER NEXT FILM.

...or was it?

The End.